For Olivia, Karen and Dave—MW

For Little Humpties Lachlan & Thomas and
Big Humpties Susanne S & John C (who helped me find my camels)
and Vivienne G for the postcards—AJ

Published in 2004 by Simply Read Books
www.simplyreadbooks.com

CATALOGUING IN PUBLICATION DATA

Wild, Margaret, 1948-
Little Humpty/ Margaret Wild;illustrated by Ann James

ISBN 1-894965-11-6

1.Camels--Juvenile fiction. I. James, Ann II. Title.

PZ10.3.W53Li2004   j813'.54   C2004-902229-6

First published by Little Hare Books, Australia.

10 9 8 7 6 5 4 3 2 1

Designed by Louise McGeachie   •   Photography by ANTART

Printed in China
Produced by Phoenix Offset

Little
HUMPTY

MARGARET WILD & ANN JAMES

SIMPLY READ BOOKS

In the hot, hot desert where the
wind whirled and the sand swirled,
lived Big Humpty and Little Humpty.

Little Humpty liked to play all day.
He liked stepping in
Big Humpty's footprints.

He liked scampering
under her tummy.

He especially liked tugging her tail,
then running off, calling,
"You can't catch me!"

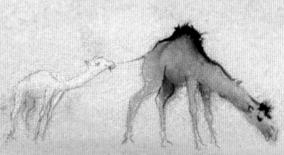

Big Humpty chased him here and there.
When she caught him, she gave him a big,
sloppy kiss and said, "You know, Little Humpty,
I love you best in all the world!"
  With a happy wriggle, Little Humpty said,
"Tell me about the world, Big Humpty. Tell me!"

So Big Humpty told him

about crocodiles and cranes,

about elephants and eagles,

about hippos and rhinos,

about fishes
and frogs…

"I'm a frog!" said Little Humpty.
"Look at me jumping in the puddles!
Come and jump, too, Big Humpty!"
So she did.

One day, after Big Humpty's tail had been tugged three times in a row, she said, "No more for now," and flopped down in the shade of the one palm tree.

Little Humpty played
on his own for a while.
He whooshed on his
bottom down a billowy,
pillowy dune.

He stuck his head
between his legs.

He ran round and
round in circles,
trying to catch his tail.

When there was absolutely nothing else
to do, he looked hopefully at Big Humpty.
But her eyes were half-closed.
  So Little Humpty went looking for
someone to play with.

"Will you play with me?"
he asked Twisty Rock.

"Will you play with me?"
he asked Scraggly Bush.

"Will you play with me?"
he asked Small Pebble.

But Twisty Rock
and Scraggly Bush
and Small Pebble didn't reply.

"Baaaa!" said Little Humpty sadly.

That night, while the wind whirled and the
sand swirled, Little Humpty snuggled up against
Big Humpty as he always did, and quickly fell asleep.

But Big Humpty was awake until the stars went out. She thought about how fast Little Humpty was growing up, and how she'd seen him trying to play with the rock and the bush and the pebble.

"Baaaa!" she said softly.

In the morning, Big Humpty said,
 "Surprise, Little Humpty! Today we're going
to walk all the way to the Great Waterhole!"
 "The Great Waterhole!" said Little Humpty.
"What will we see there, Big Humpty?"
 "What do *you* think?" asked Big Humpty.

As they began the long, hot
walk, Little Humpty said,
"I think we'll see…

…hippos. Lots and lots of rolypoly hippos rolling in the mud!"

"Goodness! Wouldn't that be wonderful!" said Big Humpty.

As they walked on and on, Little Humpty said,
"Are we there yet? Are we there yet?"
  "Not yet. There's still a long, long way to go,"
said Big Humpty.

"What else do you think we'll see at the Great Waterhole, Little Humpty?"

Little Humpty said, "I think we'll see…

…elephants. Lots and lots of elephants tramping and trumpeting!"

"I'd like to see that!" said Big Humpty.

As they walked on and on and on, Little Humpty said,
"Are we nearly there yet? Are we nearly there?"
  "Not quite," said Big Humpty.

"What else do you think we'll see at the Great Waterhole, Little Humpty?"
Little Humpty said, "I think we'll see…

…crocodiles. Lots and lots of crocodiles going snip snap, snippety snap!"

"Oooh!" said Big Humpty. "That'd be something to see!"

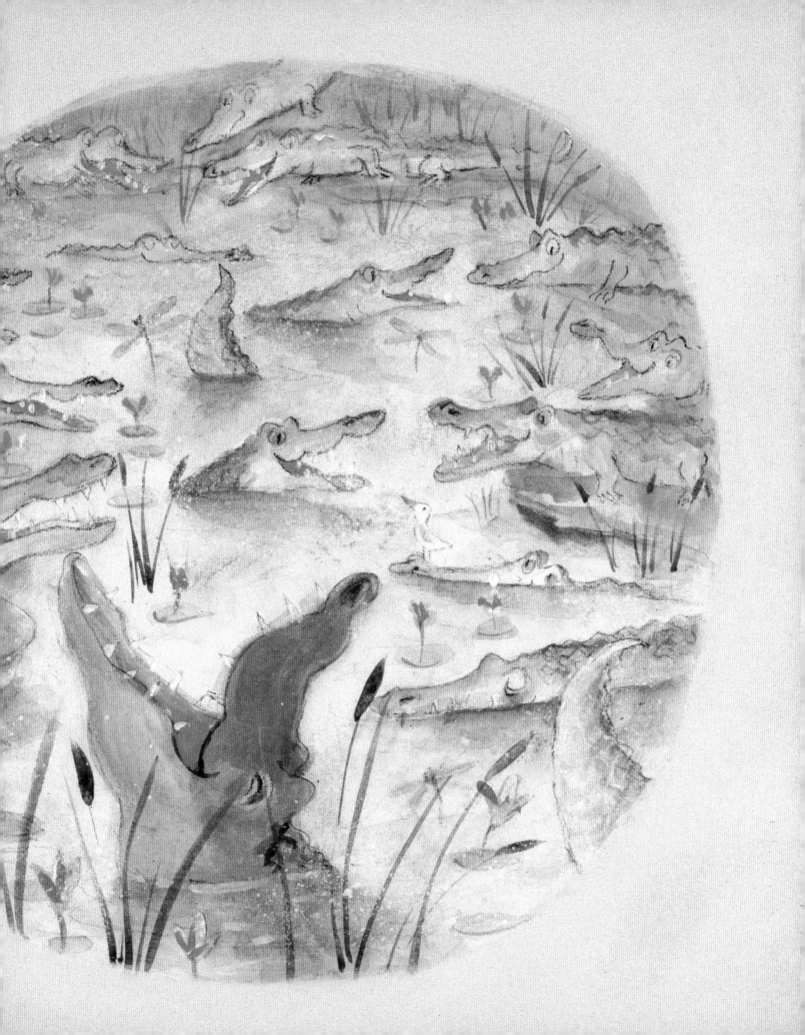

As they walked on and on and on and on,
Little Humpty said, "Are we nearly, nearly there?"
  And, at last, Big Humpty said, "Yes, we are nearly,
nearly, *nearly* there."

Then they were right there…
Little Humpty's eyes grew big.
What he saw was better than rolypoly hippos rolling in
the mud, better than elephants tramping and trumpeting,
better than crocodiles going snip snap, snippety snap…

"Oh!" said Little Humpty.
"I see lots and lots of
little humpties, just like me!"

"Lots and lots of little humpties
to play with!" said Big Humpty.
"Baaaa!" said Little Humpty happily.

Big Humpty tugged his tail. "You can't catch me!"
she said, and off they ran to the Great Waterhole.